GATHER THESE TOOLS

Learning to draw is fun, and anyone can do it—we promise!
If you just read the directions closely, and draw, draw, draw,
soon you'll be creating impressive drawings all on your own.

PENCILS

There are many kinds of drawing pencils: soft lead,
hard lead, and everything in between. It's up to you to
choose the kind you like best, but start out with an
HB pencil. The HB is right in the middle in terms of
hardness, and it's the one most artists use.

THESE ARE THE TOOLS YOU'LL NEED TO GET STARTED.

MARKERS

You'll need a lot of thin markers and at least one
thick one. Get a range of sizes and experiment
with the kind of lines they make.

PAPER

Smooth white paper is best for
drawing comics. The size of paper
doesn't matter—just remember to
be loose and fill the entire sheet
with terrific drawings. Don't hide
your artwork in a tiny corner of
the page!

ERASERS

Keep as many erasers around as you
can. Everyone makes mistakes, even
professional cartoonists!

COLORED PENCILS

Soft lead color pencils are the best
way to color your art. But you can
also use markers, crayons,
or pastels if you wish.

Okay, get
ready! It all
begins on the
next page.

STRAIGHTEDGE

A ruler or a triangle is essential for drawing
buildings and backgrounds. Always have one handy.

Some people think you need the powers of a goddess to draw. But you don't! You just need to relax and draw a few curved lines.

CURVES

Drawings are made up of many curved lines—big ones and small ones. They're easy to make, especially if you try not to think about what you're doing. Practice using your whole arm, not just your wrist. Be playful and energetic. There are no "wrong" lines at this point.

CIRCLES

Keep your arm loose, and sketch circles all over your paper.

There's no need to worry about making perfect circles yet. We're just scribbling, getting a feel for how our arms and hands work.

OVALS

Now practice drawing ovals and egg shapes.

The Lasso of Truth

Don't make a lot of scratchy, worried lines when one bold, dramatic line will do.

Drawing is fun, not careful and stiff!

Keep the shapes loose and free. Make them small or big, thin or fat. You decide!

Remember, drawing is physical activity. Get used to the rhythm of your arm and hand.

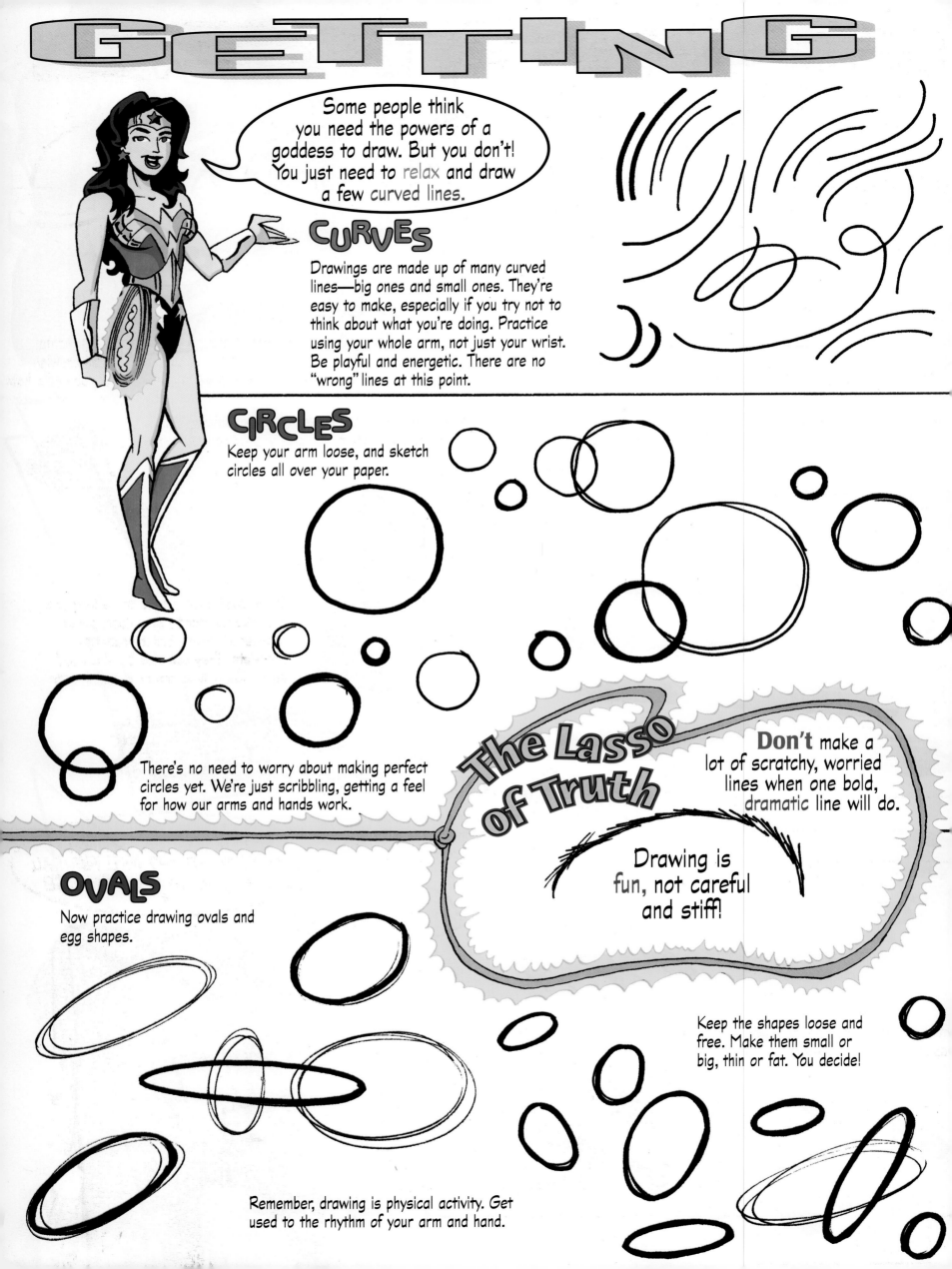

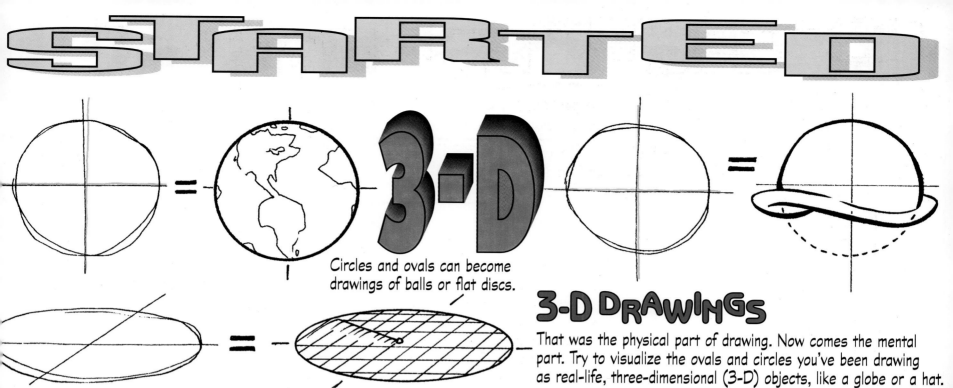

Circles and ovals can become drawings of balls or flat discs.

3-D DRAWINGS

That was the physical part of drawing. Now comes the mental part. Try to visualize the ovals and circles you've been drawing as real-life, three-dimensional (3-D) objects, like a globe or a hat.

CYLINDERS

If you draw parallel lines to connect two identical ovals (or discs) at the top and bottom, you create a cylinder, or tube.

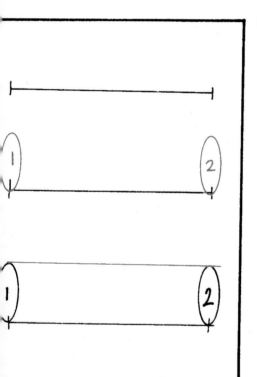

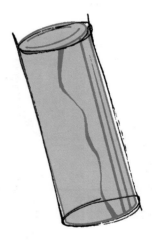

Tubes don't always have to be long and thin, like the handle of a flashlight or Wonder Woman's bullet-bouncing bracelets. They can also be short and squat, like a tuna can or a coiled lasso.

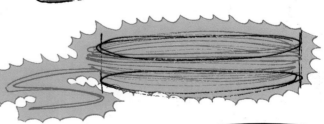

Notice how many things in the world around you look like tubes. (There are quite a lot!)

BOXES

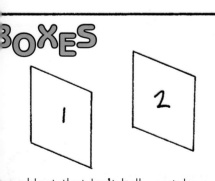

ny object that isn't ball- or tube-aped is probably box-shaped.

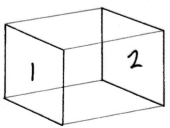

To draw a 3-D box, join two squares or diamond shapes with parallel lines.

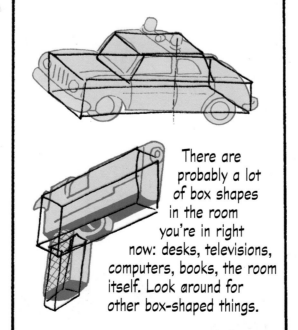

There are probably a lot of box shapes in the room you're in right now: desks, televisions, computers, books, the room itself. Look around for other box-shaped things.

SEE HOW EASY IT IS? JUST KEEP THINKING IN 3-D, AND WE'LL PUT IT ALL TOGETHER ON THE VERY NEXT PAGE!

PROPORTIONS III

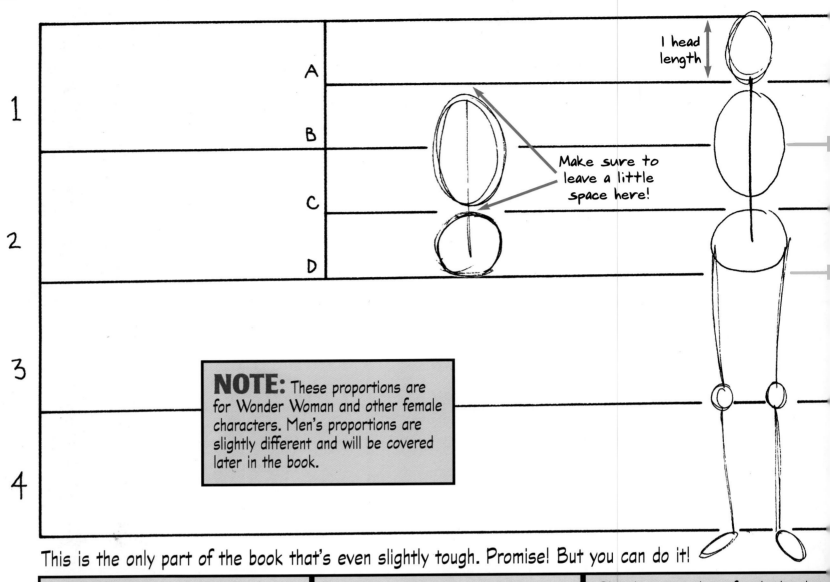

A

B

1

C

2

D

1 head length

Make sure to leave a little space here!

NOTE: These proportions are for Wonder Woman and other female characters. Men's proportions are slightly different and will be covered later in the book.

3

4

This is the only part of the book that's even slightly tough. Promise! But you can do it!

Proportion is the correct size of things in relation to other things. Not too hard, right? To make sure your proportions are correct, start with a vertical line, and divide it into four equal sections, as shown. (Make these guidelines light.) Divide the top half into four more sections. **You've got it!**

Now draw a stick figure. Make a line for the spine, starting at line A and ending halfway between lines C and D. For the upper body, or ribs, draw an egg shape that doesn't quite touch lines A or C. Then sketch a circle for the hips between lines C and D. It should rest on line D and almost touch line C.

Sketch an egg shape for the head that fits exactly inside the top sectic touching the lines at the top and bottom. The legs start at the outside of the hips and go all the way down t the ground. Score extra points if you noticed that the circles for the knee are exactly halfway between the bott of the hips and the ground.

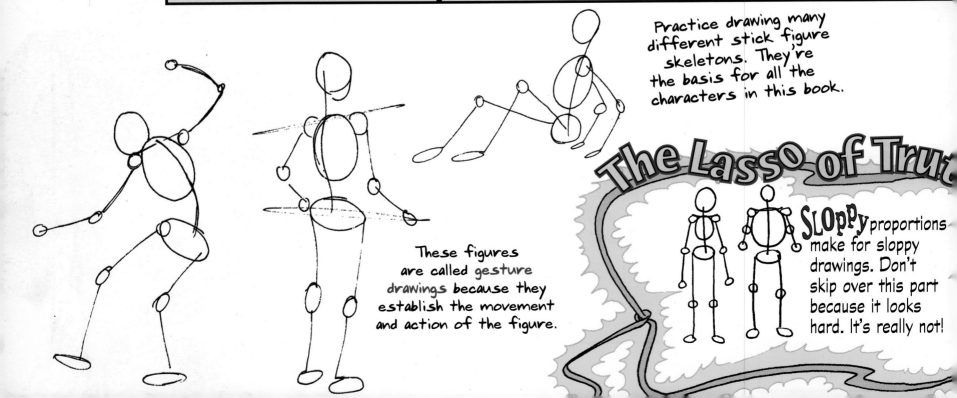

Practice drawing many different stick figure skeletons. They're the basis for all the characters in this book.

These figures are called gesture drawings because they establish the movement and action of the figure.

The Lasso of Trut

SLOppy proportions make for sloppy drawings. Don't skip over this part because it looks hard. It's really not!

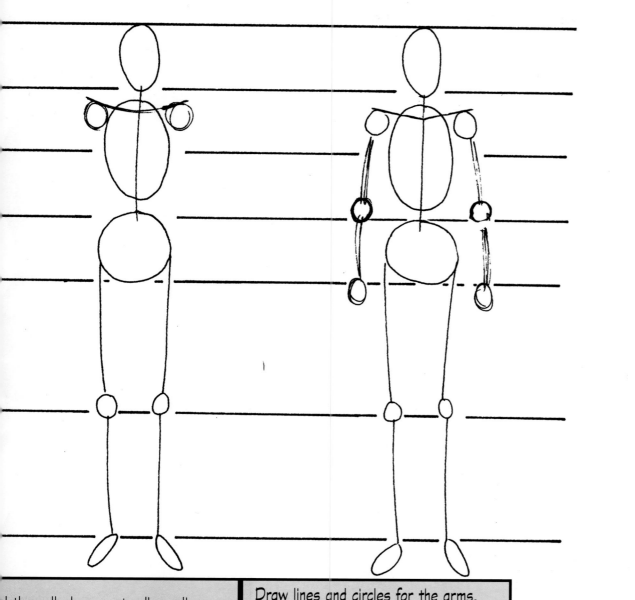

...d the collarbone, extending a line ...from both sides of the spine in the ...dle of section B. Look at how it ...les up a bit and is just slightly wider ...n the hips. For the shoulders, draw ...mall circle under each end of the ...arbone. Try to leave a small gap ...ween the circles and the ribs.

Draw lines and circles for the arms, elbows, and hands. Notice that when the arms hang down, the elbows line up with the bottom of the ribs. And the wrists, not the hands, fall exactly on line D. You artist types have probably already figured out that line D is the midpoint of the figure. Did you also notice that the figure is 8 heads tall?

WITHOUT A SKELETON, YOUR BODY WOULD LOOK ALL RUBBERY AND FALL APART. YOUR DRAWING IS THE SAME WAY. GET THIS PART RIGHT!

Is your figure 8 heads tall?

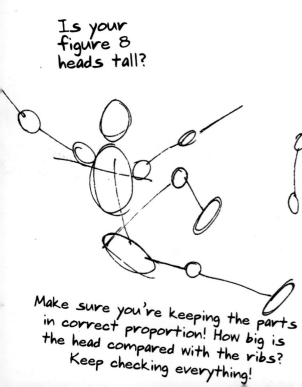

Make sure you're keeping the parts in correct proportion! How big is the head compared with the ribs? Keep checking everything!

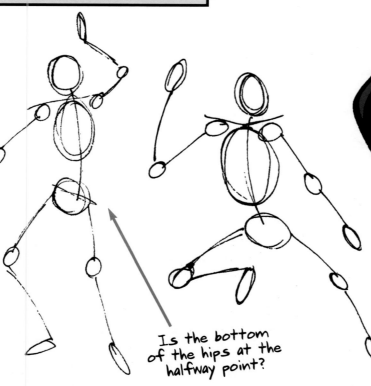

Is the bottom of the hips at the halfway point?

How to Draw the

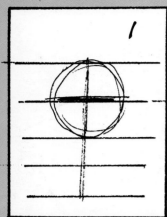   

Step 1: Begin Wonder Woman's head with a simple circle. Draw guidelines to divide it in half vertically and horizontally. Then add three more horizontal lines the same distance apart below it.

Step 2: The jaw extends down from the widest points of the circle, curving gently into the chin at the fourth line. Add the star earrings and the neck too.

Step 3: Sketch the eyes just below the second line, which is about halfway between the top of the head and the chin. The space between the eyes is equal to the width of one eye.

Step 4: The tip of the nose is placed halfway between the eyes and the chin, and the mouth is halfway between the nose and the chin. Easy to remember, huh? Draw the hair in big shapes to make it lively.

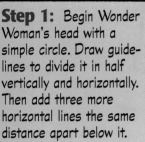 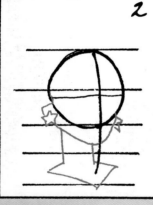 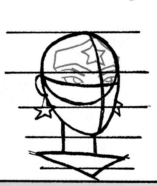 

Step 1: Start with the same circle and guidelines as before. Since Diana's head is at a three-quarter view, the center line curves to your right. Notice that you can see more of the right side of her head and less of the left side.

Step 2: Add the jawline, curving down almost to the fourth line. In this view, only her right ear is visible. Notice where the vertical lines of the neck meet the curved lines of the face.

Step 3: The eyes are placed on the curved horizontal guideline. When drawing the tiara, notice that it takes up the whole top third of the face.

Step 4: The nose goes halfway to the chin on the vertical center line. The full lips are placed just below the third line. Once again, big shapes make up the hair.

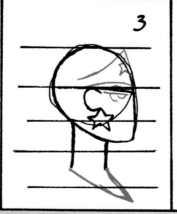 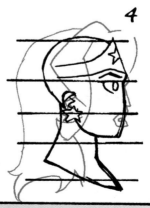

Step 1: For the profile, start with the circle shape and the same horizontal guidelines, but make the circle slightly wider than it is tall.

Step 2: The jaw slopes down gently to the fourth line. The ear goes right above where the jaw connects to the back of the circle.

Step 3: Add the eyes just below the second line. Notice that the tiara still takes up the top third of the face.

Step 4: When drawing the hair in profile, try to think of it as the same hair you're drawing in the frontal and three-quarter views. Check to see that the hair shapes look the same, except they are turned slightly.

FACE and HEAD

Try drawing these heads at different angles. It helps if you think of the head in 3-D—like a ball. Being able to draw the face and head from different views is important for creating the exciting action scenes coming up later in the book.

TRY THE SAME STEPS WITH ME!

I'M YOUNGER, SO I HAVE SLIGHTLY DIFFERENT PROPORTIONS. OBSERVE CAREFULLY.

WHAT'S DIFFERENT ABOUT OUR FACES? WHAT'S THE SAME?

EIGHT HEADS ARE BETTER THAN ONE. KEEP PRACTICING!

STOP!
LET ME GIVE YOU A HAND!

Hands come in a lot of different sizes and proportions, but there are some basic rules that will get you started with a female hand (we'll get to men's hands later). Once these rules are solidly in your head, your characters will grab, wave, and point convincingly.

Start with a circle. Divide it in half vertically and horizontally. This will be the palm of the hand.

Draw an oval in the lower right section for a right hand, in the lower left section for a left hand.

Add a smaller oval on top of the first one to make the thumb. Notice that both ovals are at about a 45° angle.

Add a pointed curve and vertical lines for the fingers. The fingers are long and thin, and they taper to a point.

3rd **1st**

The first and third fingers are usually about the same length. The pinky is the smallest (or they'd think of a better name for it!).

The palm is just slightly wider than the four fingers. Notice that the wrist is much narrower than the palm.

Knuckle

Knuckle

Wrist

The side view is a bit trickier. Start with a triangle. Extend the top line (index finger) twice as long as the bottom line (thumb).

Now let's beef up the thumb and finger by putting some flesh on those bones!

Halfway along the thumb side is the knuckle. Same for the finger.

The wrist attaches close to where the thumb connects. The other fingers join at the knuckles on top.

Study your own hand when adding details. Real artists observe closely; they don't just guess!

YES!

Knuckles are smooth lines.

NO!

Not like this. Bumpy knuckles may be realistic, but they're not "animated style."

NO!

Knuckles line up in gentle curves, not straight lines.

Wonder Woman's long fingers come to a point.

YES!

More HANDS

Focus on the rhythms and curves of the hands.

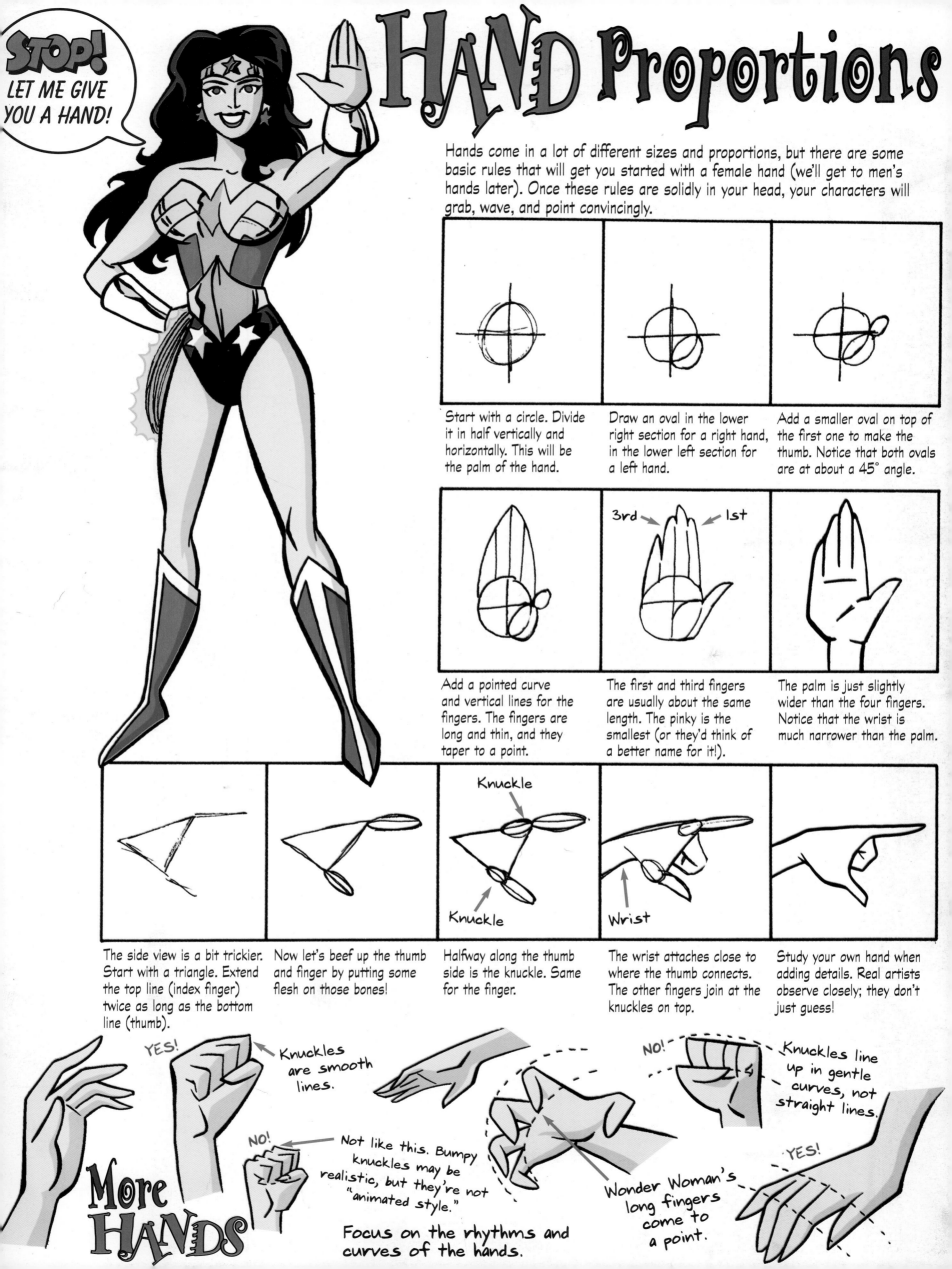

NO, I'M NOT DIRECTING TRAFFIC.

I'M DEMONSTRATING THE TWO MOST IMPORTANT THINGS ABOUT FORESHORTENING:

THINGS APPEAR TO GET BIGGER AS THEY COME TOWARD YOU,

AND THE LINES OF THE SIDES OF THINGS COMING TOWARD YOU APPEAR SHORTER.

CHECK OUT MY HANDS AND FEET. WHICH ONES ARE BIGGER?

Big

Small

Lines of leg shorter

Big

Small

Lines become shorter

YOU'LL SEE WHAT I MEAN WHEN I TIP OVER THIS TUBE SHAPE.

THE SAME THING HAPPENS WHEN I TIP MY HEAD FORWARD...

To start off, the tube is upright. You're seeing it more or less straight on, so the top and bottom ovals of the tube are about the same size.

As the tube starts to tip forward, the top of the tube is closer to you than the bottom is—right? The top oval looks slightly bigger than the bottom oval, which is farther away.

Now the top and the bottom of the tube are rounder, and the top appears much larger and closer than the bottom. Also notice that the sides of the tube are getting shorter.

In this position, the top of the tube is much, much larger than the bottom, and the lines for the sides are practically gone. That's foreshortening!

THE LENGTH OF MY FACE APPEARS SHORTER, AND THE TOP OF MY HEAD LOOKS LARGER THAN THE BOTTOM. SEE HOW LOW MY FACE IS ON MY HEAD?

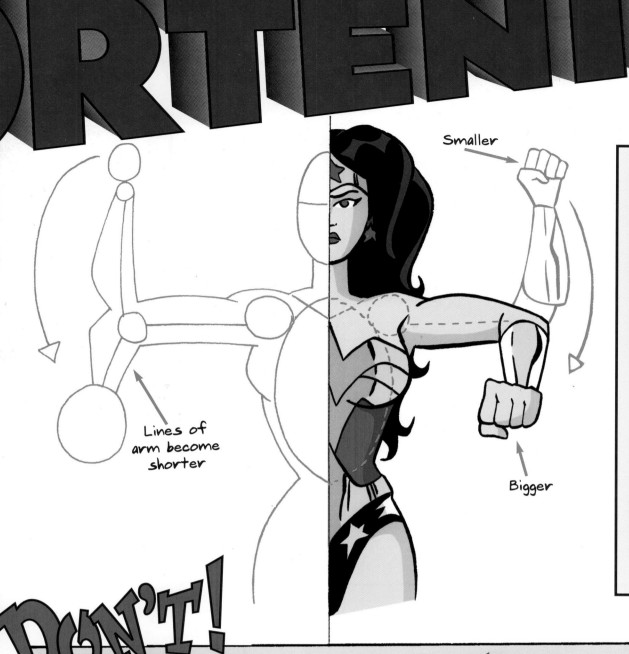

Smaller

Lines of arm become shorter

Bigger

Foreshortening a figure isn't hard to do. You just have to think of the figure in terms of simple shapes, like the tubes and the boxes we've already drawn. If you think of the arms and legs as tubes and the shoulders, elbows, hands, knees, and feet as ball or box shapes, it's easy to foreshorten the figure the same way we just did with the tube!

Look closely at the drawing to the left. See how, as the arm bends toward you, the lines of the sides of arm become shorter? See how the hand that is closer to you is larger?

DON'T!

Don't make the smaller shape the one in front. Remember, things get BIGGER as they come closer to you and smaller as they go farther away.

This isn't a tube—it's a traffic cone or a megaphone!

This isn't a box—it's a cowbell!

MOOOO!

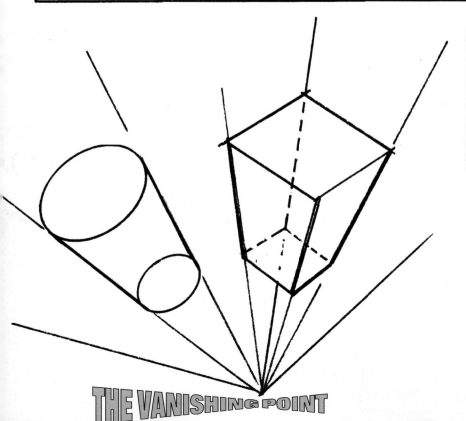

THE VANISHING POINT

PERSPECTIVE & THE VANISHING POINT

When Diana throws her magic lasso far away, you'll notice that it becomes not just a bit smaller but a LOT smaller. If she could throw it a few miles away, it would eventually be too small to see. The point where it gets so small that it appears to vanish is called the **vanishing point** (makes sense—right?). Remember that all objects in a drawing get smaller as they move toward the vanishing point. Look around you for things that seem to get smaller or vanish in the distance—like train tracks, long walls, or sidewalks.

I'M SURE YOU'RE EAGER FOR YOUR FIRST POSE!

Check these spaces!

Lightly and loosely, with easy movements and a light touch of the pencil, sketch in the four most important forms first—spine, ribs, hips, and head. These forms give the body weight and balance. Be sure to check your proportions to make sure everything is the right size and in the right place.

For balance, the hips should be centered over the feet. The hips are the **center of gravity** in a woman's body. If they aren't lined up correctly, she will look as if she's falling over. Keep checking those proportions!

Once the gesture drawing is correct, it's time to **flesh out** the rest of the character.

Curved
Straight

Curved
Straight

An important aspect of this style of drawing is the way the arms and legs are drawn. One side of each part is always curved, while the other side is straighter.

Observe the details carefully. How high are her boots? How far up the arm do the bracelets go? How long is her hair? Then it's time to ink over the lines and color!

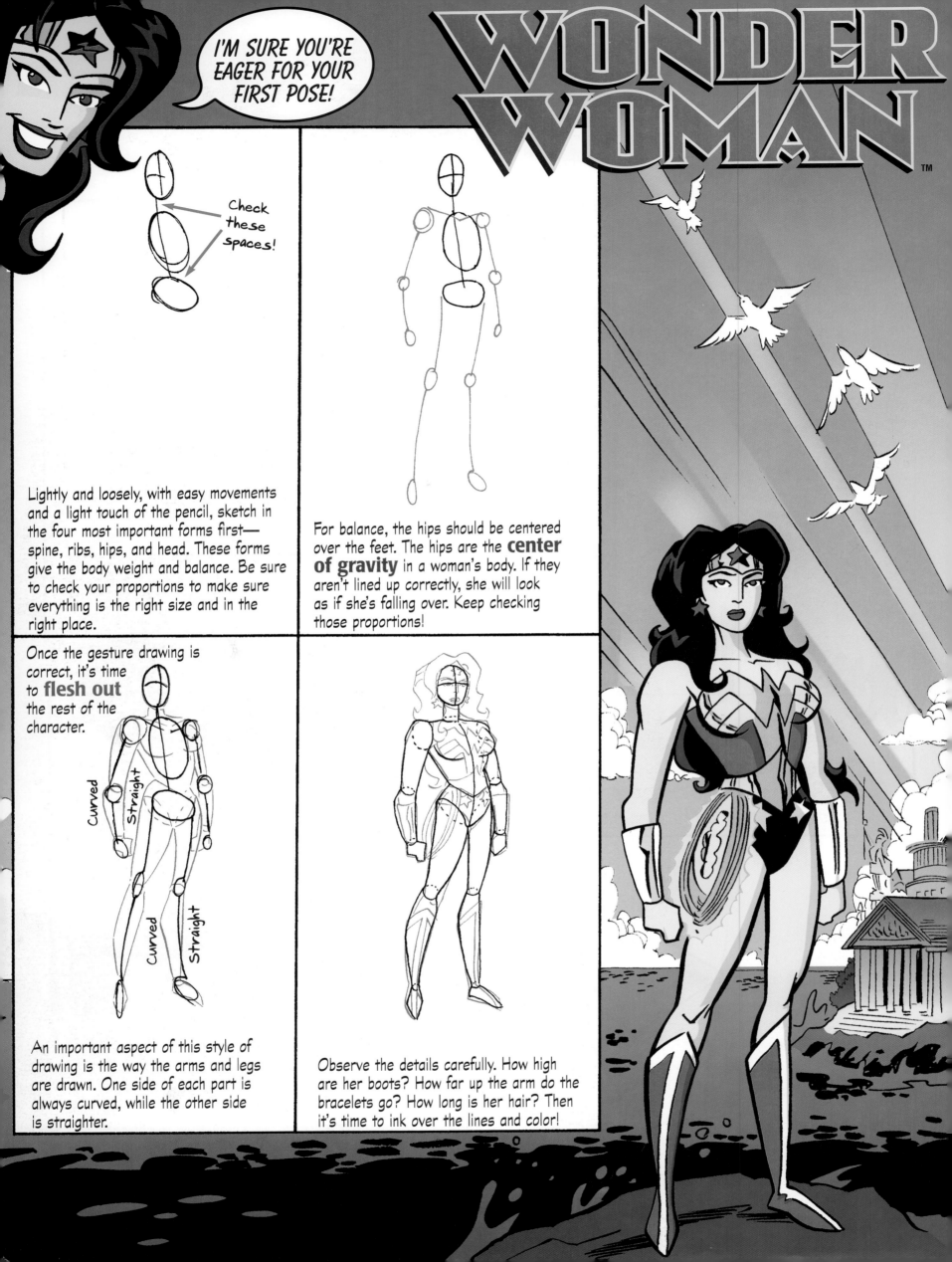

FLY Like an Eagle

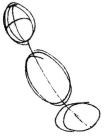

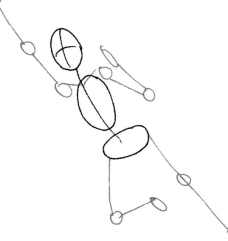

Start with a light sketch for the gesture drawing. The same four basic shapes lead us off—spine, ribs, hips, and head, in that order.

You don't have to put the head directly above the hips in this drawing; she's flying. She doesn't have a center of gravity when she's defying gravity in the first place!

Now put some meat on those bones! Keep checking the proportions every time you draw. Is the space from the hips to the knees 2 heads long? Are the hips wider than the ribs?

When you have all the forms sketched in correctly, you can finish your drawing in ink, and then color it in.

The Golden Lasso

Look at the curve of Diana's spine in this pose. She's leaning forward, so the spine has to curve forward substantially. The bend in the spine doesn't change the basic construction, though.

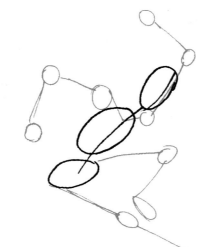

The arms and legs come next. Even though her head is in front of her left arm, you still need to draw the entire arm. This is called **drawing through,** and artists do this so all the parts are positioned correctly.

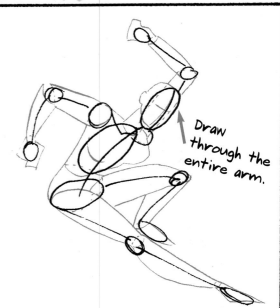

Draw through the entire arm.

Flesh out the forms, but continue to draw through so the arm is drawn in the correct proportions. Make your lines light so you can erase them later.

Add the final details. Keep the hair flowing in big, easy shapes. Now you'll be covering up the left arm—but see how it's drawn correctly, in the right position? When you're done, ink carefully and color.

THE AMAZON WARRIOR

HERE ARE SOME NOTES ON WONDER WOMAN'S COSTUME

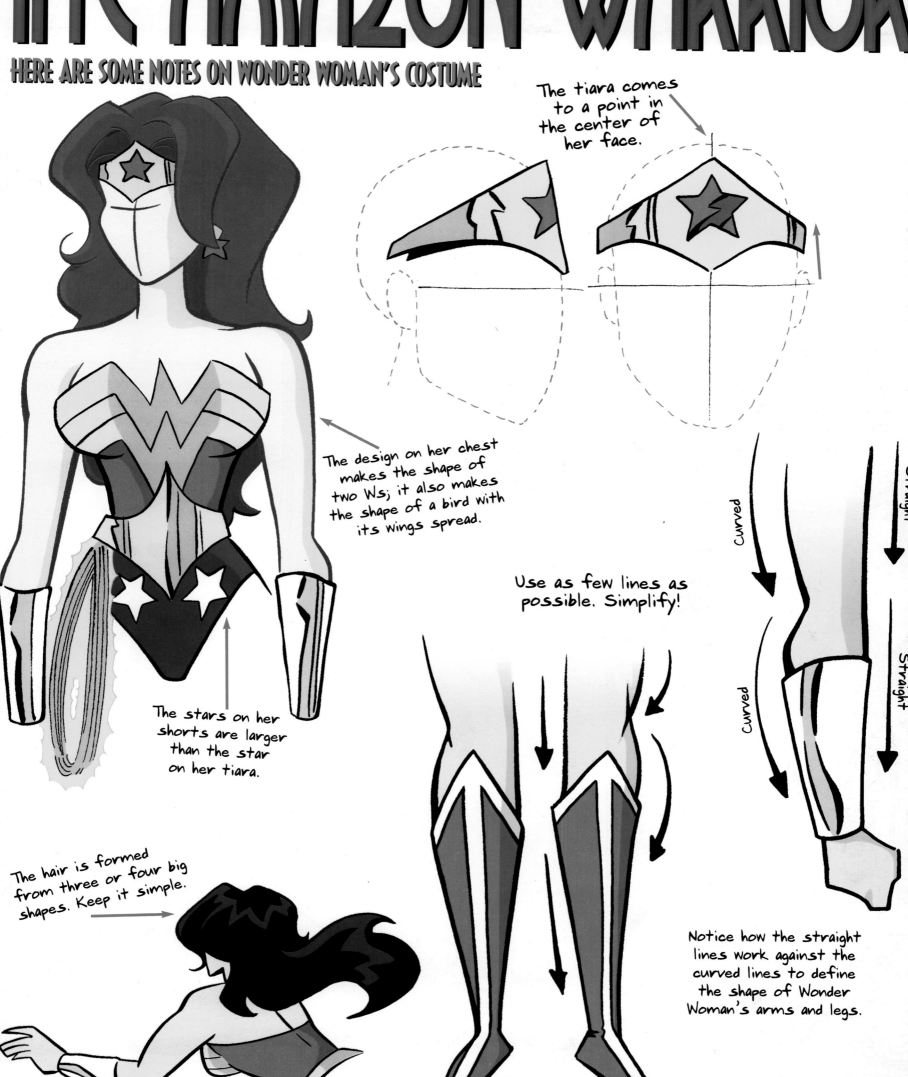

The tiara comes to a point in the center of her face.

The design on her chest makes the shape of two Ws; it also makes the shape of a bird with its wings spread.

The stars on her shorts are larger than the star on her tiara.

Use as few lines as possible. Simplify!

Curved

Straight

Curved

Straight

The hair is formed from three or four big shapes. Keep it simple.

Notice how the straight lines work against the curved lines to define the shape of Wonder Woman's arms and legs.

Great Hera, Give Me Strength!

Here Diana is lifting a huge, heavy weight, which shifts her center of gravity to directly underneath the weight. We have to draw her spine to show that it's taking all the weight, and so we make it bend backward. Never forget the all-important sketching order: spine, ribs, hips, and head.

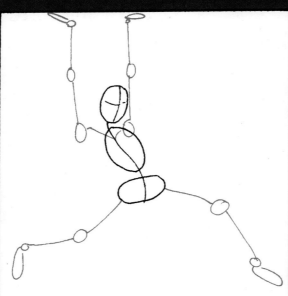

Add the legs and arms in a way that maintains the balance and weight. Notice that her hips line up over the center of the space between her feet.

The arm joins the body from the back. Remember this when fleshing out the sketch with fuller forms. Look for those straight/curved relationships too.

Time to ink and color. We suggest that you use "heavy" colors.

TIME FOR A LITTLE "Bullets and Bracelets!"

The Lasso of Truth

When making highlights on metallic surfaces, try to give your lines a smooth, playful feeling.

Make bold lines, S-curves, and zigzags.

Women are usually much more flexible than men are. You can really see the curve of Diana's back in this shot.

Even though you can't see Diana's legs, you still need to think about what's going on outside the frame. She has to look balanced.

When filling out the large forms, try to see them as simple shapes. Use a straightedge to draw the trails of the bullets—don't cheat!

UP, UP, and Away!

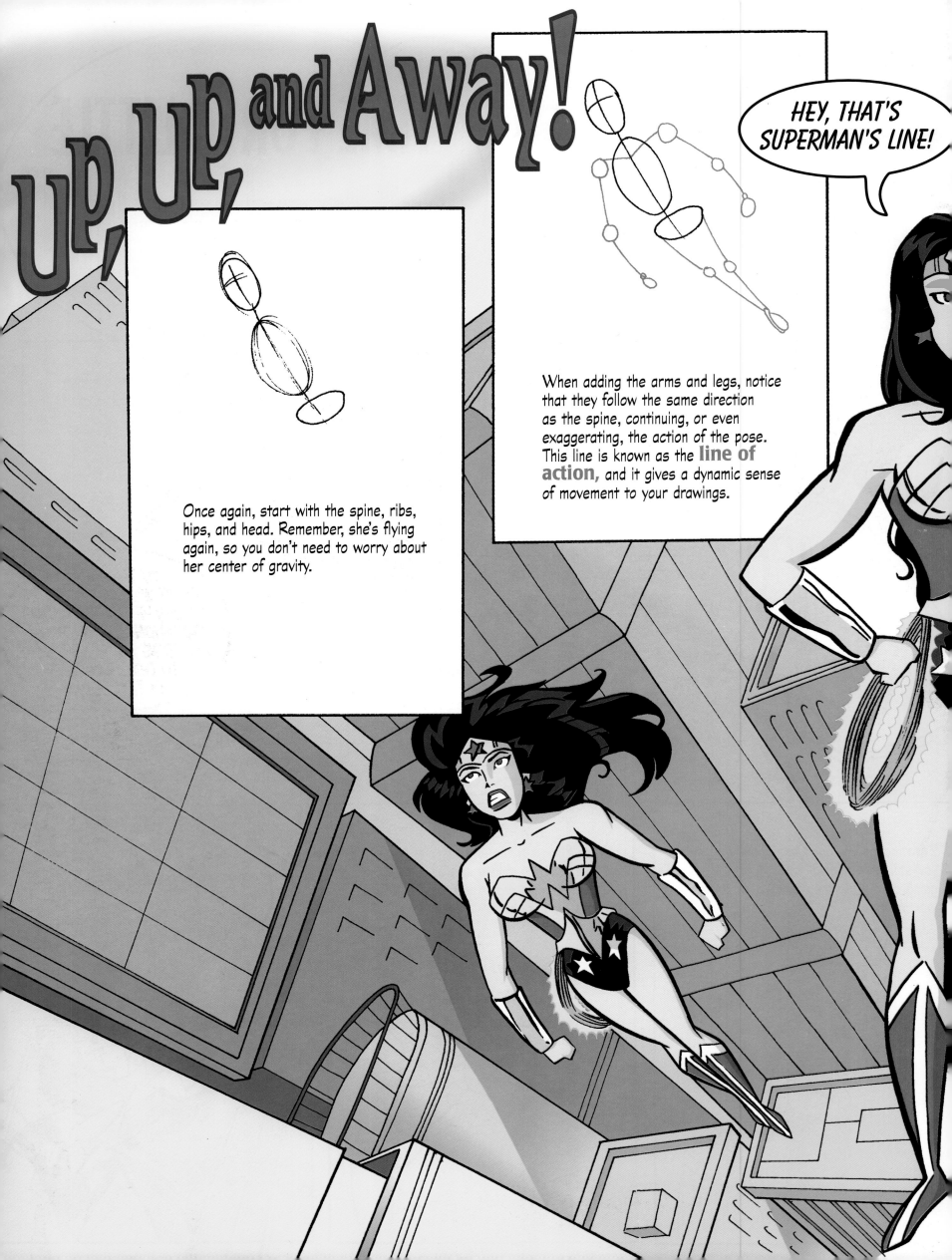

Once again, start with the spine, ribs, hips, and head. Remember, she's flying again, so you don't need to worry about her center of gravity.

When adding the arms and legs, notice that they follow the same direction as the spine, continuing, or even exaggerating, the action of the pose. This line is known as the **line of action,** and it gives a dynamic sense of movement to your drawings.

HEY, THAT'S SUPERMAN'S LINE!

Big

Small

When fleshing out this pose, keep in mind that Wonder Woman is flying toward you, so you will need to use the rules of perspective and foreshortening to keep her in correct proportion.

See how the head is much bigger than the feet? That's foreshortening in action! Now ink your drawing, and color it in.

Can you find the line of action in all of the poses in this book? It's easy!

BY THE WAY, I DON'T WEAR MY COSTUME ALL OF THE TIME. PUT SOME VARIATION INTO YOUR ART BY ADDING YOUR OWN IDEAS TO THE DRAWINGS IN THIS BOOK!

See how the line of action makes this running pose more dynamic?

THE MALE

THREE BASIC DIFFERENCES IN SKELETAL STRUCTURE

1. The first difference is obvious—men tend to be larger, broader, taller, and heavier than most women. You can see it in the skeleton; a man's is larger on average. Of course, the world is filled with people of all shapes and sizes, so there are tiny men and huge women (actually, Wonder Woman is taller than the average man!), but it tends to be the other way around.

2. The second difference is that men usually have wide upper bodies with small hips, while women usually have wide hips with slender upper bodies. Exactly the opposite! That puts a man's center of gravity (the heaviest part of his body) in his chest, and a woman's center of gravity in her hips. It's important to keep this difference in mind when drawing men and women.

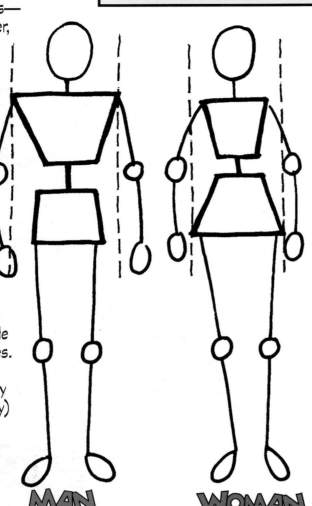

MAN   WOMAN

WOMAN   MAN

3. A man has a fairly straight, rigid posture, with just a slight pelvic tilt. On the other hand, a woman has a strong, noticeable tilt in her hips from front to back. It's in opposition to the slight backward tilt in her back. When a woman stands up straight, there is a gentle arch to her posture.

On average, a man's body may be taller than a woman's, but it's still 8 heads tall!

THE PROPORTIONS STILL WORK OUT BECAUSE TALLER PEOPLE HAVE SLIGHTLY TALLER HEADS.

FORM

MEN, LIKE WOMEN, COME IN A VARIETY OF SHAPES AND SIZES. HERE ARE SOME GENERAL RULES FOR MAKING YOUR MALE CHARACTERS LOOK "MANLY."

BASIC DIFFERENCES IN FACIAL STRUCTURE

ZEUS

Heavier brow

Men can have facial hair.

HERMES

Nose tends to point down. It is heavier and stronger than a woman's nose.

Mouth and lips are a thin line and often wider than a woman's mouth. Certainly, men have lips, but it's best not to emphasize them too much.

Steve Trevor

Don't draw eyelashes.

Face is wider. So is the neck.

Jason Blood

Eyebrows are thicker. They can even be a little bushy.

Men have more sculpted cheekbones; they're not smooth.

MEN'S HANDS

Remember, no bumps for the knuckles.

Wrist is only slightly smaller than palm.

Fingers are square at the ends.

Hair on fingers and knuckles really suggests a man's hand!

Practice drawing many hand gestures using your own hand as a model. Getting the hand to look good is very important.

MIKE SCHORR, G.C.P.D.

THEY SAY THERE'S NEVER A COP AROUND WHEN YOU NEED ONE, BUT THIS IS ONE COP I CAN ALWAYS COUNT ON TO BE THERE FOR ME.

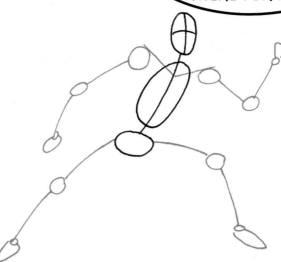

Begin with spine, ribs, hips, and head, just as usual. But, when adding the arms and legs, the center of gravity becomes important again. Remember, a woman's center of gravity is in her hips, but a man's is in his chest.

But you will notice here that Mike's center of gravity is off a little bit. If you draw a line straight down from his chest, you will see that it is just to the right of center of the space between his legs. He is leaning forward, so his left leg is bent slightly—it's carrying all of his weight.

Flesh out the figure, but don't worry about the clothes yet. It's important to have a solid figure in correct proportion before worrying about the details, such as his jacket or his gun.

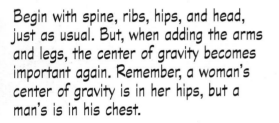

Now add the final touches. Remember that the pants and jacket are loose fitting, so they will bunch up at the elbows and knees. Just add a few wrinkles, and you're ready to ink and color.

HERACLES

Heracles is one of the mythical Greek gods, renowned for his great strength. Here, he's making short work of a brick wall! He puts all his weight into the blow, so he's leaning forward, with his head in front of his ribs. His ribs are also in front of his hips, but everything still lines up on the spine.

Remember your foreshortening when drawing the arms; make sure that the left hand, which is farther forward, is larger than the right one, which is farther back. Notice also that the right leg is bent because he is leaning forward into the punch. Don't forget to draw through for all the parts covered by his left arm!

Small

Big

You're probably wondering why we're drawing the feet, since, in the final drawing, they are hidden behind the brick wall. It's important to always draw the whole figure so that you can be sure everything is correct before adding anything that would cover it up—whether it's clothes or a brick wall!

Now you're ready to add the final details, including the hair, clothing, and face. See how the hair sweeps up and falls back into the line of action? This helps make him look as if he's leaping right at you! When you're ready, go ahead and ink and color.

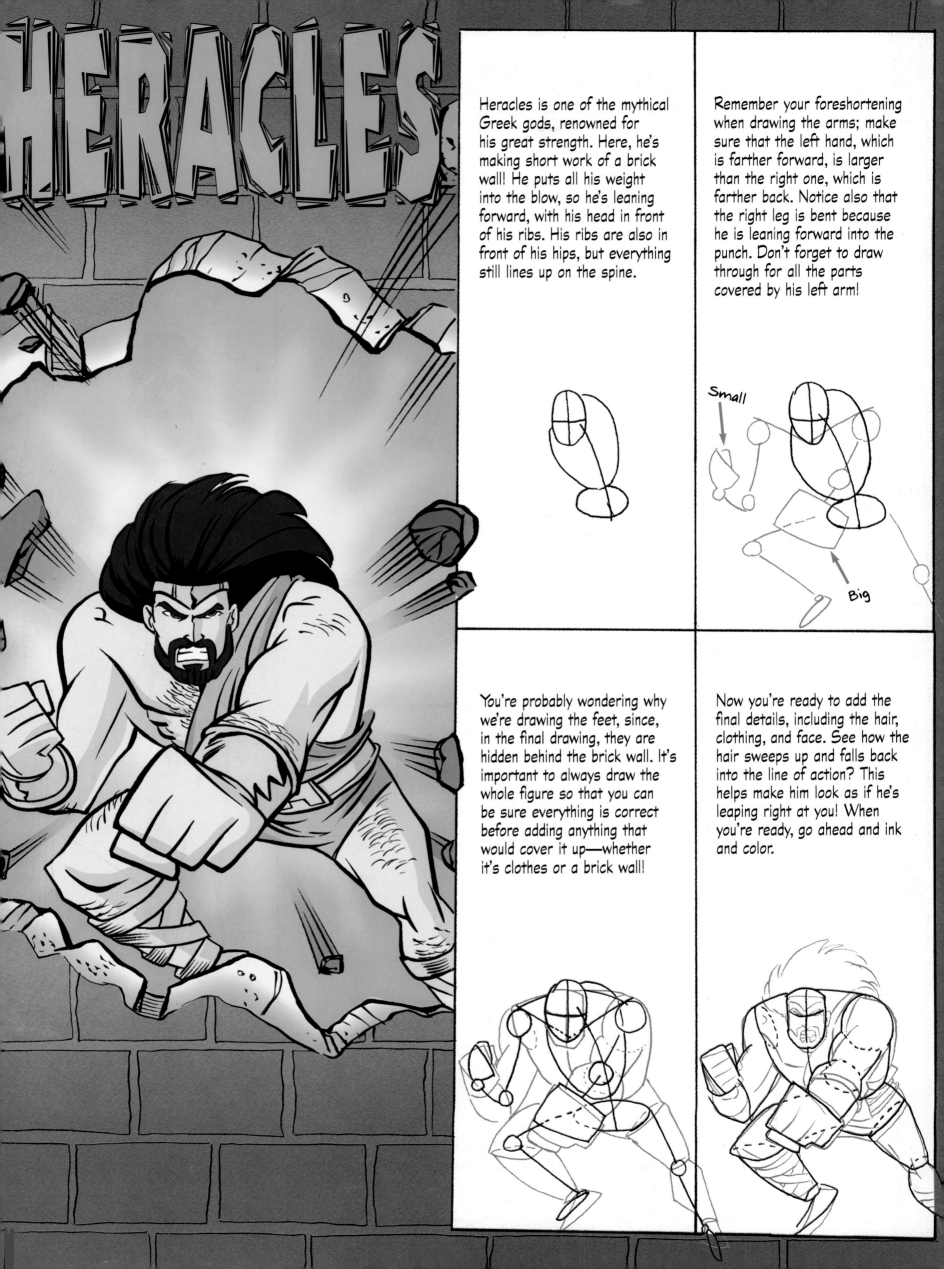

THIS IS MY MOTHER, THE QUEEN OF THE AMAZONS.

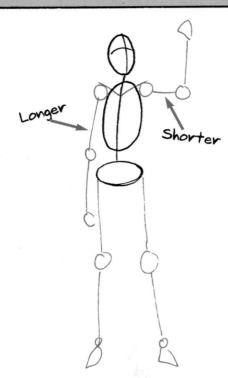

Longer

Shorter

Begin as usual, with the spine, ribs, hips, and head. Make the spine a nice, straight line, so Queen Hippolyta will have a tall, regal stance.

Watch the foreshortening on the left arm. See how her left arm is shorter than her right one?

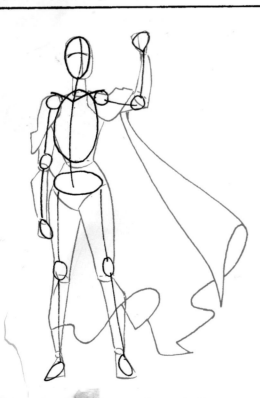

Make sure you finish the figure before you start sketching in the clothing. For effect, her robe and cape are moving slightly from a light breeze. This detail adds movement to a character who is really just standing still.

When adding the details, check to be sure that all the lines of the wrinkles flow in the same direction—the wind blows in only one direction at a time! Now you're ready to ink and color.

DONNA TROY

DONNA USED TO CALL HERSELF WONDER GIRL, AND, ALTHOUGH SHE DOESN'T HAVE HER POWERS ANYMORE, SHE'S STILL A HERO!

Begin with the spine, ribs, hips, and head, remembering to stay loose and use your whole arm when drawing. There is a lean to this figure, because it's in a dynamic running pose.

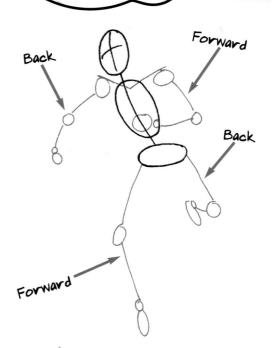

Back   Forward   Back   Forward

See how her left arm and right leg are both coming forward? And how her right arm and left leg are both going back? In this position, the arms and legs are in **opposition** to each other. Opposition adds life to your drawings!

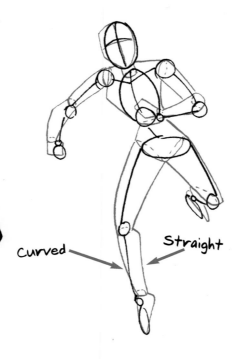

Curved   Straight

Flesh out the figure, remembering to use curved lines with straight lines to form the shapes. Don't forget your foreshortening either!

Add the clothes, and draw her hair sweeping back. Then ink and color, and you've got a heroic figure, even without a costume!

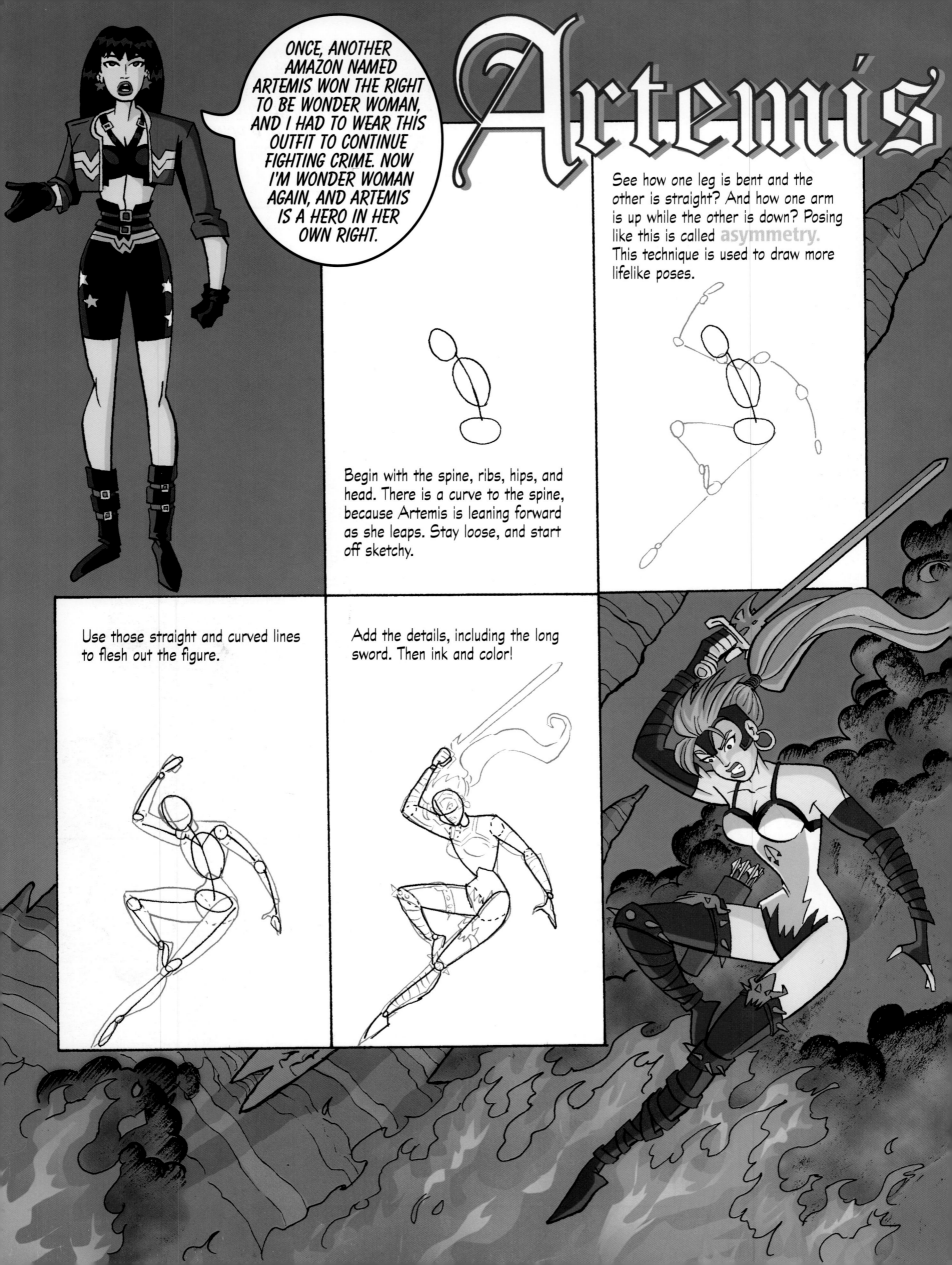

Jason Blood and THE DEMON ™

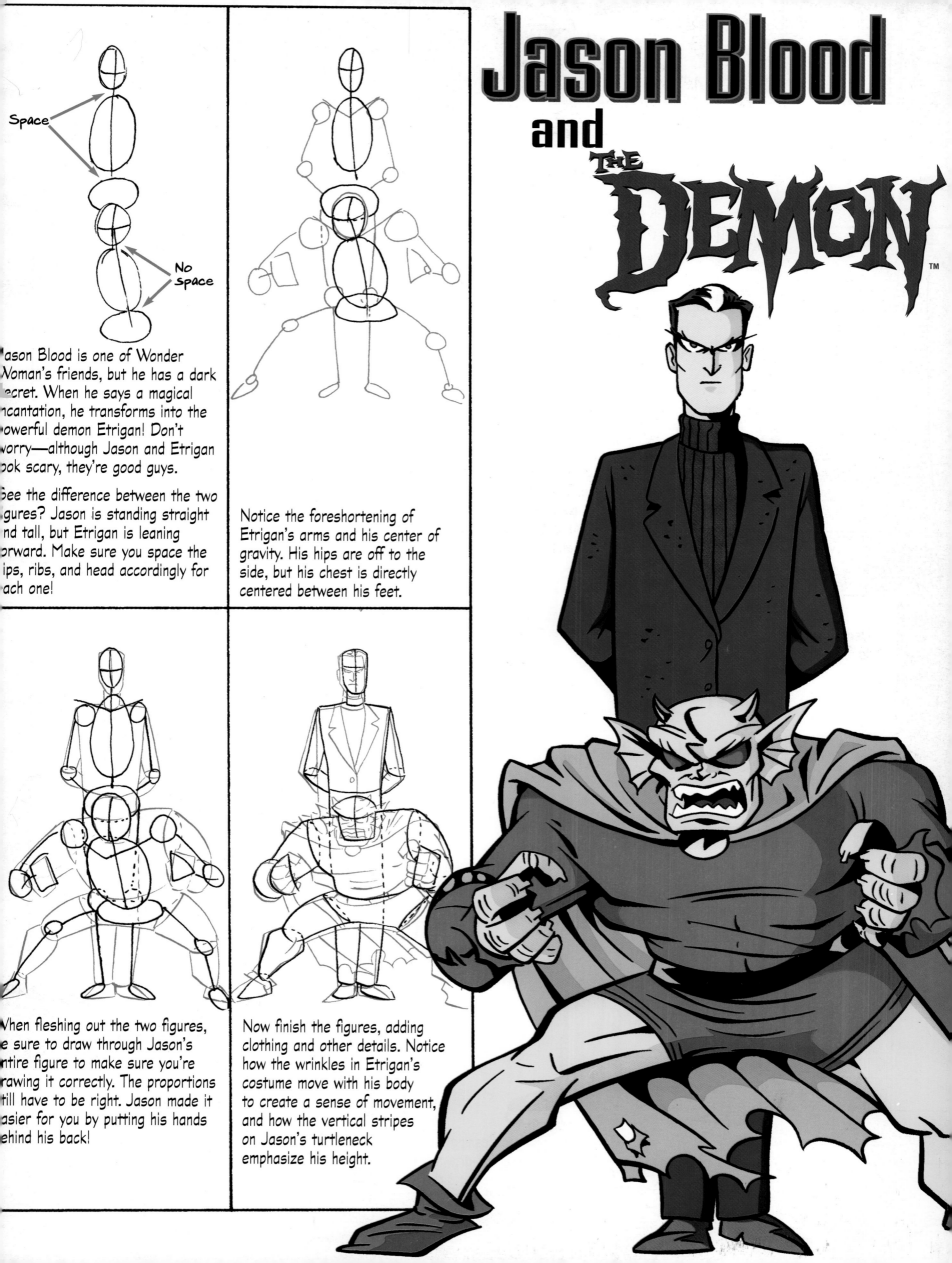

Space

No space

Jason Blood is one of Wonder Woman's friends, but he has a dark secret. When he says a magical incantation, he transforms into the powerful demon Etrigan! Don't worry—although Jason and Etrigan look scary, they're good guys.

See the difference between the two figures? Jason is standing straight and tall, but Etrigan is leaning forward. Make sure you space the hips, ribs, and head accordingly for each one!

Notice the foreshortening of Etrigan's arms and his center of gravity. His hips are off to the side, but his chest is directly centered between his feet.

When fleshing out the two figures, be sure to draw through Jason's entire figure to make sure you're drawing it correctly. The proportions still have to be right. Jason made it easier for you by putting his hands behind his back!

Now finish the figures, adding clothing and other details. Notice how the wrinkles in Etrigan's costume move with his body to create a sense of movement, and how the vertical stripes on Jason's turtleneck emphasize his height.

Helena and Cassandra Sandsmark

WITH HER NEWFOUND POWERS, CASSIE FANCIES HERSELF THE NEW WONDER GIRL, BUT HER MOTHER, HELENA, WON'T STAND FOR IT.

Drawing these two figures will give you a good idea of the differences between characters of different ages. Cassie is a lot shorter than her mother, but you still have to keep her in proportion.

See how Helena's arms and legs are longer than Cassie's? Details like this are important when drawing different characters, because no two people are alike. Just remember the rules, and each figure will turn out right!

When fleshing out the figures, remember that a full-grown woman has more curves than a young girl.

Cassie's hairstyle and big eyes lend her a more youthful appearance, while Helena's glasses and thicker lips make her look more mature.

Steve and Etta Trevor

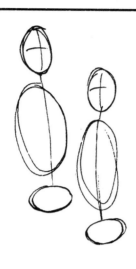

Two of the first friends Wonder Woman made when she came to America were Steve Trevor and Etta Candy. She watched them grow closer and fall in love. Now they're happily married and ready to show you the differences between men and women in one drawing.

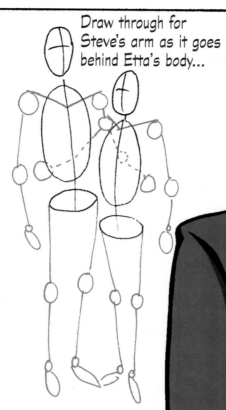

Draw through for Steve's arm as it goes behind Etta's body...

...and Etta's arm where it goes behind Steve's—even if the arms won't be visible in the final drawing.

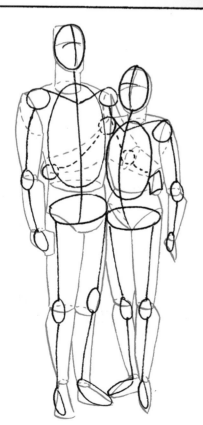

Flesh out the figures. Remember the differences between men's and women's proportions!

Etta is a bit heavier than Wonder Woman, so her face is rounder, and her body and neck are a little bigger.

NOW FOR SOME VILLAINS!

Cheetah, one of Wonder Woman's deadliest archenemies, is perched in a tree, ready to attack! Following the curve of the spine, the ribs and head slightly overlap because she's leaning forward.

Start loose and easy with the spine, ribs, hips, and head. Circe is reclining on some pillows, so she has a relaxed curve to her spine.

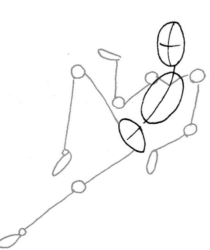

She's leaning back, putting her weight on her left arm, so the left arm should be bent, supporting her weight. Her right arm is turned up as a perch for one of the mutated animals she controls.

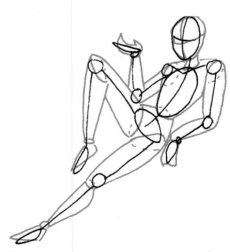

Notice the asymmetry between Circe's arm and legs. Doesn't she look relaxed? She's probably plotting some evil scheme.

Circe

THESE PAGES CONTAIN SOME OF THE DEADLIEST VILLAINS I'VE EVER FOUGHT.

You've probably already noticed where her center of gravity is, right? Add the arms and legs, always remembering to draw through the areas that are covered.

Cheetah doesn't wear clothes, because, like the animal, she is covered in fur. Cheetahs are sleek cats, so their fur tends to stick out only at the joints, such as the knees and elbows. This makes her look furry—but not too furry.

Now you're ready to ink and color. Remember that cheetahs have lots of spots—and don't forget the tail!

Now add the final touches, including the big black raven perched on her finger. Then ink and color.

NERON

Neron is sitting on his throne, leaning forward slightly. This means that when you draw the hips, ribs, and head, the head is in front of the ribs, but the ribs are still above the hips.

When drawing the arms and legs, remember the rules of foreshortening. Notice how short his thighs are? And you can't even see his right forearm!

When fleshing out the figure, remember to draw through all the foreshortened body parts. Neron is big—so use big, bold strokes

Now add the final details, and you're ready to ink and color one of the most dangerous villains ever. Be careful!

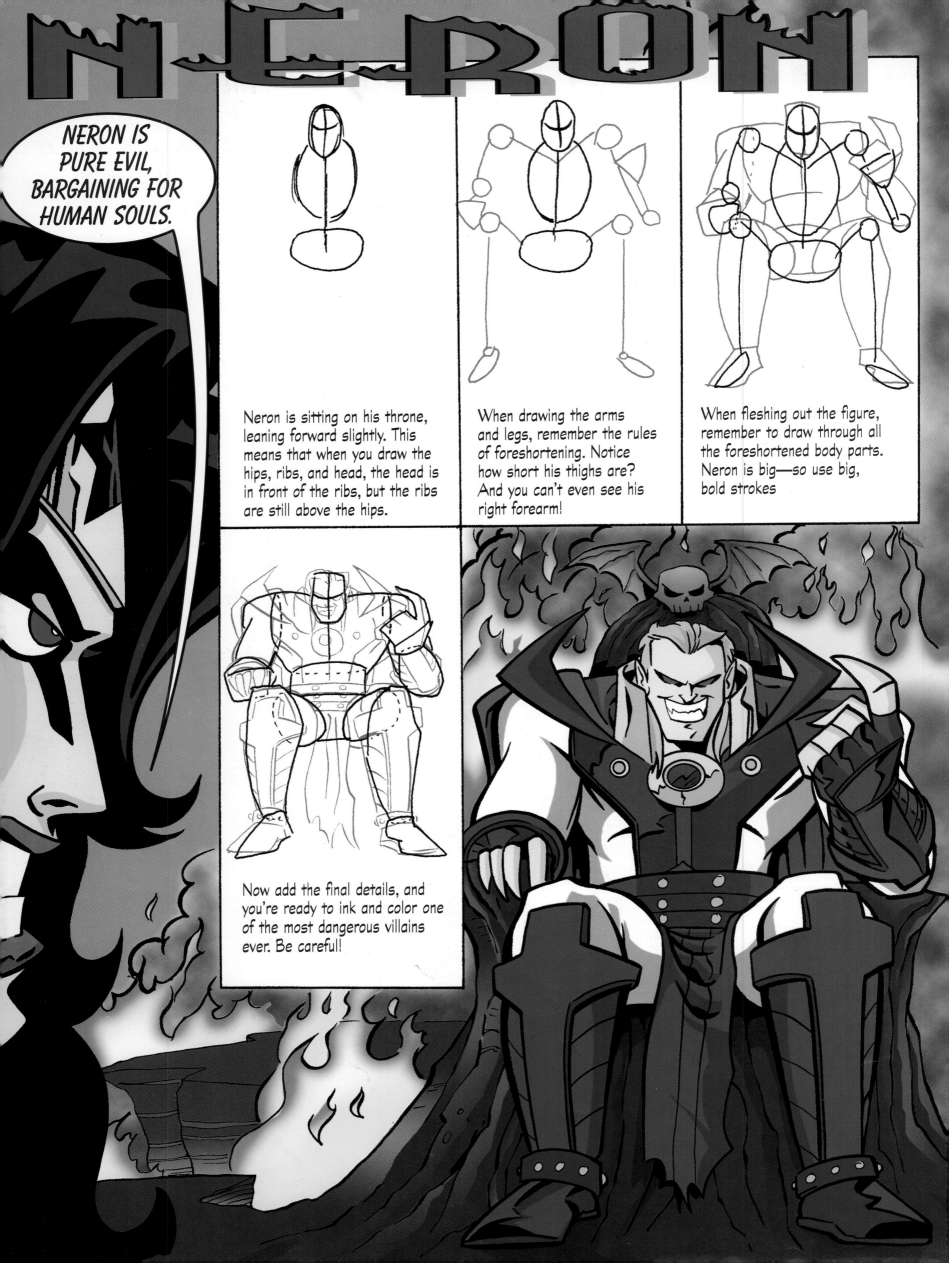

ARES

MOST OF THE GREEK GODS ARE BENEVOLENT, BUT NOT THE GOD OF WAR.

You know the drill by now—spine...ribs...hips...head.

Ares is standing in a triumphant pose, with his arms raised high. Notice how one arm is bent more than the other. That's asymmetry coming up again!

Even though Ares has a helmet on, you still have to start with the oval for the head, and draw the helmet over it.

Add some final touches, and it's time to ink and color the god of war!

PERSP

TO DRAW IN PERSPECTIVE, YOU NEED TO THINK ABOUT THE HORIZON LINE, WHERE THE SKY MEETS THE GROUND. IT'S ANOTHER WAY OF SAYING "EYE LEVEL."

Remember when we learned that lines moving from the foreground toward the background merge at a vanishing point? Well, almost all vanishing points are located on the horizon. (The exceptions will come later.)

HORIZON LINE

VANISHING POIN

The horizon line is where the viewer's eye level would be if he or she were standing inside the picture.

Only objects that are parallel to one another go toward the same vanishing point. If they're at different angles, like the tubes above, they go toward different vanishing points.

ONE-POINT PERSPECTIVE

One-point perspective is when there is only one vanishing point in a drawing, and all the parallel lines in the drawing go toward it—just like this drawing of Helena Sandsmark's office at the museum. The lines of the objects in the room—the walls, the cabinet, the desk, even the rug—all meet at the same vanishing point. Look closely at the drawing, and you'll get the idea!

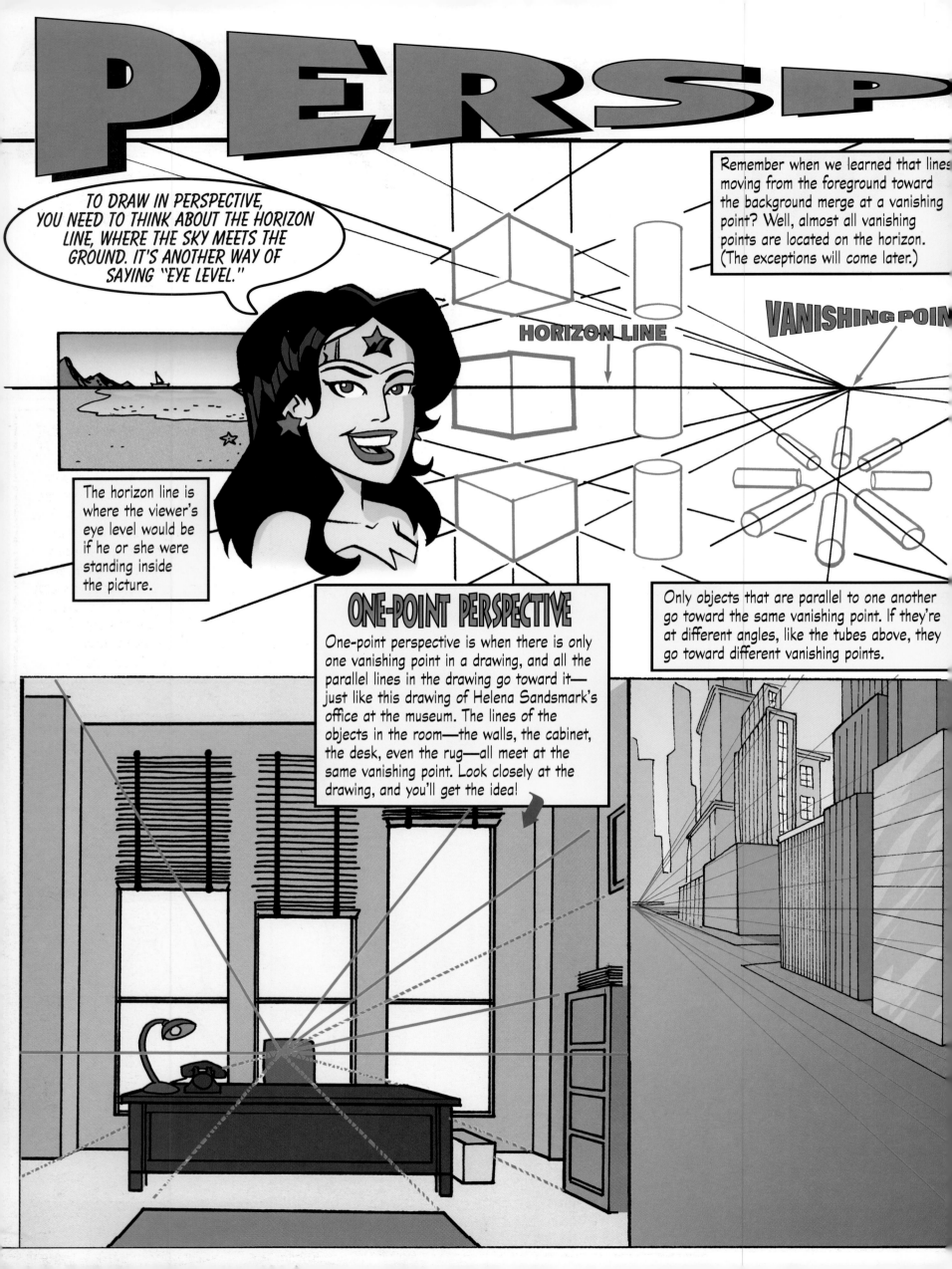

CIRCLES IN PERSPECTIVE

It's easier than you'd think to draw circles in perspective. First draw a square, and then draw a circle inside the square. Easy—right? Then draw a square in perspective by making the parallel lines go toward a vanishing point. As you change the angle of the square (by changing the vanishing point), the shape of the circle will change along with it.

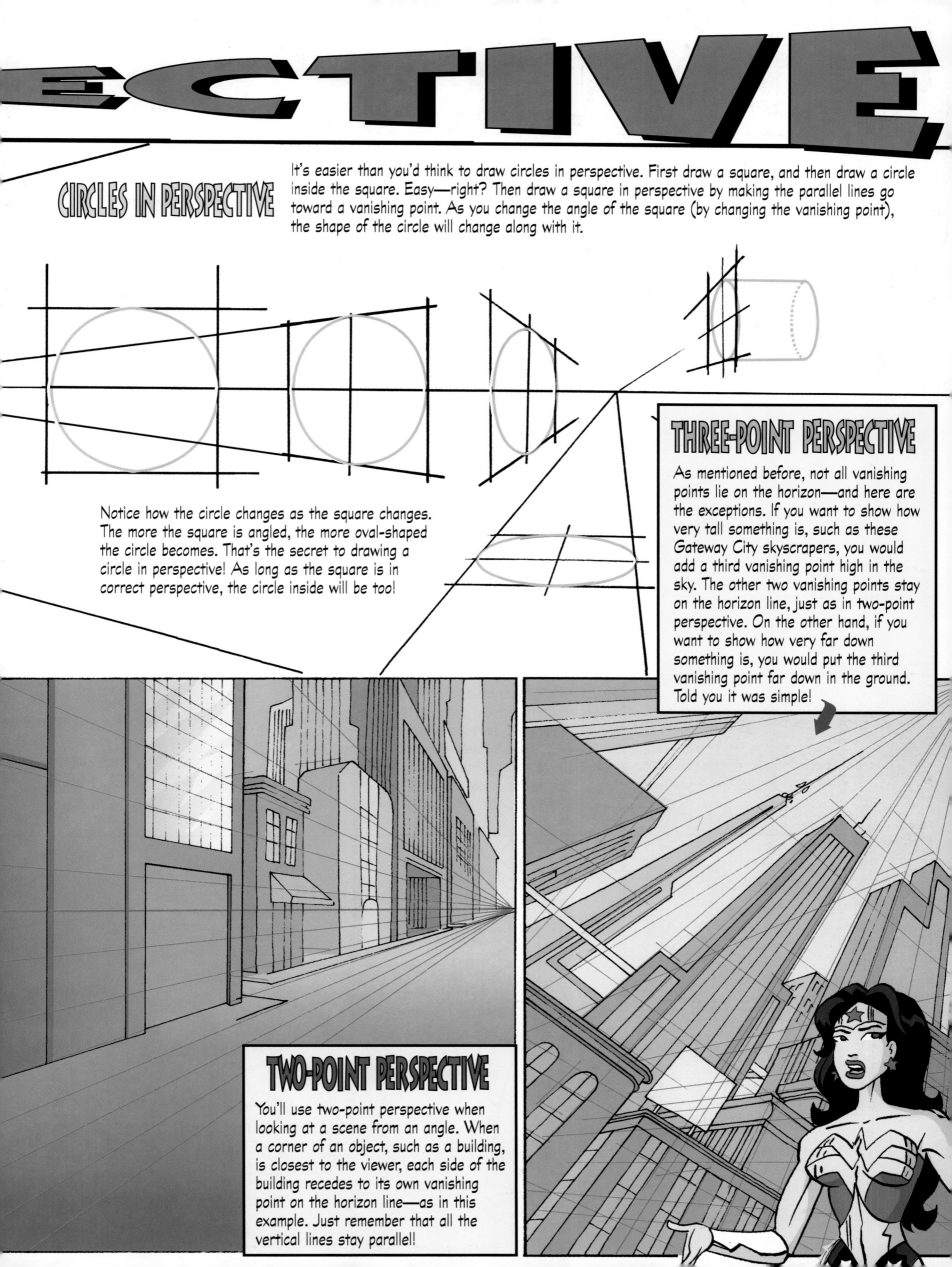

Notice how the circle changes as the square changes. The more the square is angled, the more oval-shaped the circle becomes. That's the secret to drawing a circle in perspective! As long as the square is in correct perspective, the circle inside will be too!

THREE-POINT PERSPECTIVE

As mentioned before, not all vanishing points lie on the horizon—and here are the exceptions. If you want to show how very tall something is, such as these Gateway City skyscrapers, you would add a third vanishing point high in the sky. The other two vanishing points stay on the horizon line, just as in two-point perspective. On the other hand, if you want to show how very far down something is, you would put the third vanishing point far down in the ground. Told you it was simple!

TWO-POINT PERSPECTIVE

You'll use two-point perspective when looking at a scene from an angle. When a corner of an object, such as a building, is closest to the viewer, each side of the building recedes to its own vanishing point on the horizon line—as in this example. Just remember that all the vertical lines stay parallel!

8 heads tall

Buildings and desks aren't the only things that can be drawn in perspective. Anything can—even people! This may seem difficult because of all the rounded shapes, but it's really very easy.

All you have to do is make sure the joints are parallel and that they can be drawn to the same vanishing point. Ankles, knees, wrists, elbows, and shoulders should all line up, as in the drawing above. It also helps if you picture the head, ribs, and hips as boxes.

Ta-Dah! Using a vanishing point makes foreshortening easier—don't you think? That's because you don't have to guess where all the parts go.

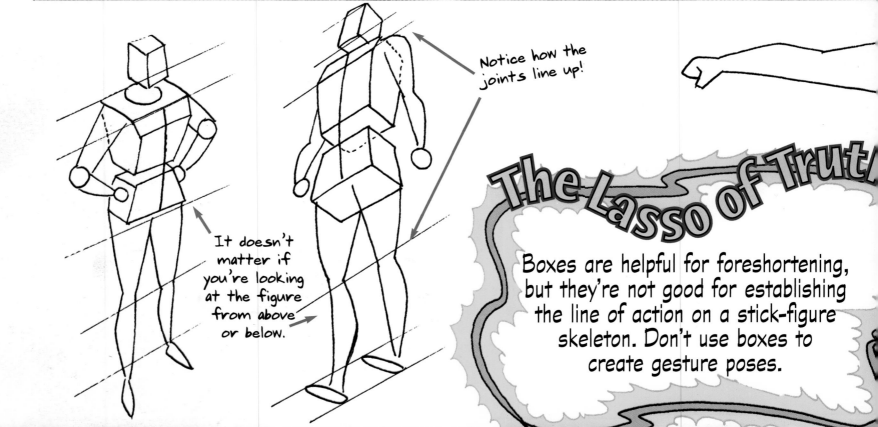

Notice how the joints line up!

It doesn't matter if you're looking at the figure from above or below.

The Lasso of Truth

Boxes are helpful for foreshortening, but they're not good for establishing the line of action on a stick-figure skeleton. Don't use boxes to create gesture poses.

Next Question:

How do you put more than one figure in the same drawing? The rules of perspective say that closer figures are bigger, and figures farther away are smaller. But how do you know how much bigger or how much smaller?

There's a complicated set of rules you could use, but here's an easy shortcut. All you have to do is place the horizon line through the same part of each figure. In the example above, the horizon line is going through the figures' ankles.

Here, the horizon line is going through all the figures' hips. To get the perspective right, make sure that the characters are always positioned on the horizon in the same place—it doesn't matter how big or how small the figures are. Notice that Wonder Woman is the biggest figure here, so she appears closest.

If the figures are below the horizon, it gets a little trickier. First draw Wonder Woman the size you want. Then count how many heads below the horizon line she is. Then simply draw Steve and Cassie the same number of heads below the line, making sure to use their own head sizes for measuring. See? It's easy!

If you think of the body parts as boxes, it'll be easier to put them into perspective at any angle!

BET YOU NEVER KNEW DRAWING COULD BE THIS EASY!